I0624125

Brrémaud, Frédéric,
Little tails on the
farm : with Chipper & Sq
2017.
33305243327354
sa        09/18/18

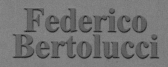

Federico
Bertolucci

Little
TAILS

on the Farm

with
Chipper & Squizzo

## WRITTEN BY
# Frédéric Brrémaud

## ILLUSTRATED BY
# Federico Bertolucci

Translation by Mike Kennedy

**LITTLE TAILS** on the Farm (Volume 5)

First Printing, 2017

ISBN: 978-1-942367-53-6

First published in France by Editions Clair De Lune

Library of Congress Control Number: 2017952242

Little Tails on the Farm (Volume 5), published 2017, by The Lion Forge, LLC.
Copyright 2017 Frédéric Brrémaud and Federico Bertolucci. All Rights Reserved.
LITTLE TAILS™ Frédéric Brrémaud and Federico Bertolucci.
LION FORGE™, CUBHOUSE™, MAGNETIC™, MAGNETIC COLLECTION™, and
the associated distinctive designs are trademarks of The Lion Forge, LLC.
Printed in China.

WWW.LIONFORGE.COM

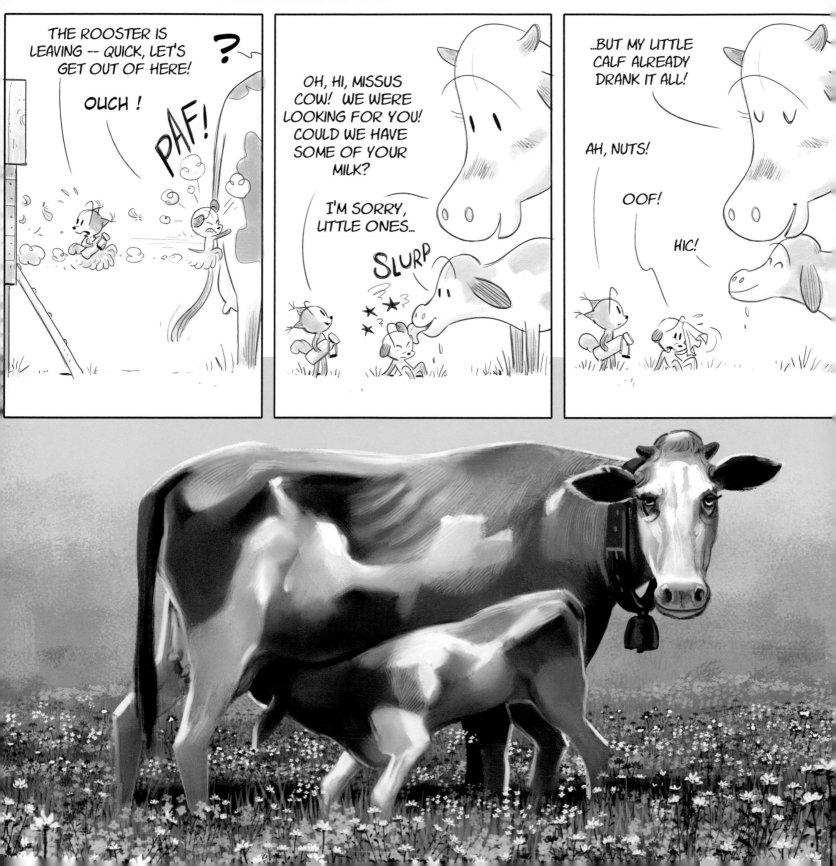

FOLLOW ME! I'VE GOT IT ALL UNDER CONTROL!
RIGHT BEHIND YOU, BUT...
...I'M GONNA PUT ON SOME SUNGLASSES. THAT BIG CHICKEN IS AS SHINY AS A STREETLIGHT!
THAT'S NOT A BIG CHICKEN -- THAT'S A PEACOCK! HE SPREADS HIS TAIL FEATHERS TO SHOW OFF HOW BEAUTIFUL HE IS!

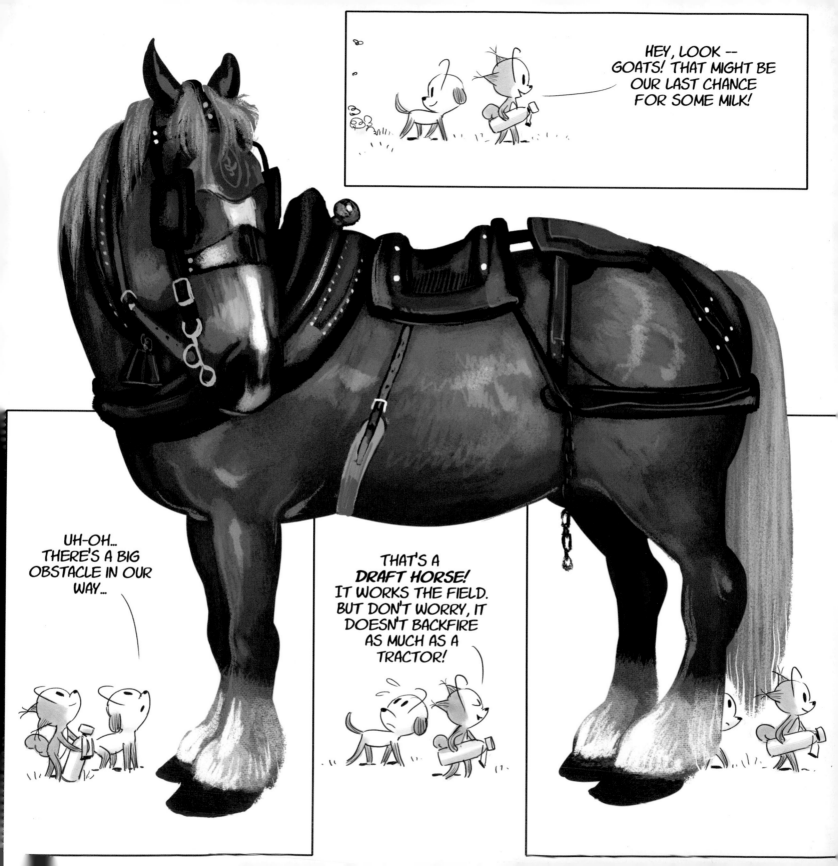

# CAT

LIKE ALL FELINES, THE REGULAR HOUSE CAT IS REALLY TALENTED AT NIGHT. IT'S NOT THAT THEY CAN SEE IN PITCH-BLACK DARKNESS, BUT THEY CAN SEE SIX TIMES BETTER THAN HUMANS IN THE DARK! THAT'S BECAUSE THEY HAVE A SPECIAL LAYER OF TISSUE INSIDE THEIR EYES CALLED "TAPETUM LUCIDUM" THAT HELPS THEM SEE WHEN THERE IS VERY LITTLE LIGHT IN A ROOM. IT IS THIS "TAPETUM LUCIDUM" THAT SOMETIMES MAKES IT LOOK LIKE A CAT'S EYES ARE GLOWING!

I KNOW IT'S DARK BUT YOU COULD HAVE USED YOUR SENSE OF SMELL!

I HAVE A STUFFY NOSE...

SNIF !

# HORSE

DID YOU KNOW YOU CAN TELL WHAT KIND OF MOOD A HORSE IS IN BY LOOKING AT HIS EARS? WHEN HE IS CALM, HIS EARS ARE OPEN AND RELAXED. IF HE IS AFRAID, THEY ARE TURNED BACKWARD TO LISTEN BEHIND HIM. AND IF HIS NOSE IS PINCHED, TOO, BE CAREFUL -- HE'S ANGRY! AND IF HIS HEAD IS HELD HIGH AND HIS EARS ARE UP AND POINTING FORWARD HE IS DEFINITELY PAYING ATTENTION!

# RABBIT

YOU KNOW THOSE BIG FEET RABBITS HAVE? WELL THEY'RE NOT JUST THERE TO HELP THEM HOP FAR AND RUN FAST (ALTHOUGH THAT IS VERY IMPORTANT, TOO)! THEY HELP RABBITS WARN EACH OTHER WHEN DANGER IS NEAR BY THUMPING THE GROUND WITH THEIR BIG FEET! SINCE RABBITS DON'T HAVE FANGS OR CLAWS OR HARD SKIN, THEIR MAIN TOOL FOR SURVIVAL IS... MAKING LOTS OF BABY RABBITS! THEY CAN HAVE SEVERAL LITTERS OF BABY RABBITS (CALLED "KITS") EVERY YEAR!

# BEES

DID YOU KNOW THAT BEES COMMUNICATE WITH EACH OTHER BY DANCING? IT IS A VERY COMPLEX LANGUAGE, AND WE DON'T KNOW WHAT ALL OF THE MOVES IN THEIR STRANGE BALLET MEAN, BUT SOME SCIENTISTS THINK THAT IF THEY FLY IN IN A FIGURE-EIGHT PATTERN, THAT MEANS THEY FOUND FOOD. AND IF THE BEE WIGGLES HER TAIL, THE FOOD IS MORE THAN 300 FEET AWAY. OTHERWISE, THERE IS GOOD STUFF NEARBY!

# PEACOCK →

ORIGINALLY FROM INDIA, THE PEACOCK IS A VERY OLD AND RESPECTED BIRD. WHEN THE MALE DISPLAYS HIS TAIL FEATHERS IN A BIG FAN BEHIND HIM, IT IS HARD FOR FEMALES TO RESIST... SO COLORFUL AND BRIGHT! THEIR TAILS ARE MADE OF SEVERAL KINDS OF FEATHERS: THE ONES THAT LOOK LIKE EYES ARE CALLED "OCELLI," AND THE MORE OF THESE THEY HAVE, THE MORE ATTRACTIVE THEY ARE TO THE FEMALES.

ARE YOU TRYING TO TELL ME SOMETHING?

YES! I KNOW WHERE THE COOKIES ARE HIDDEN!

TCHIP
TCHIP
TCHIP

# PIG

EVERYONE THINKS THE PIG IS A DIRTY ANIMAL, BUT IT'S NOT TRUE! IN FACT, THEY ARE ACTUALLY VERY CLEAN! WELL, EXCEPT THAT THEY ROLL AROUND IN THE MUD. YEAH, THAT IS PRETTY CONFUSING... YOU SEE, THE PIG'S SKIN IS VERY SENSITIVE, SO THEY ROLL IN WET MUD TO KEEP THEIR SKIN MOISTURIZED, LIKE USING LOTION. ALSO, LOTS OF LITTLE BUGS LIKE TO CLIMB IN THEIR HAIR, AND THE BEST WAY TO GET RID OF THE BUGS IS A GOOD MUD BATH! SO THEY'RE NOT JUST BEING MESSY... THEY'RE ACTUALLY BEING SMART!

WANNA GO FOR A SWIM?

UH...

MAYBE ANOTHER TIME...

## FOX

EVEN THOUGH WE DIDN'T SEE ANY FOXES IN THIS JOURNEY, THEY ARE QUITE OFTEN HIDING NEAR FARMS. THEY ARE THOUGHT OF AS SNEAKY, CLEVER THIEVES, MOSTLY BECAUSE THEY HAVE A REPUTATION FOR SNEAKING INTO CHICKEN COOPS AND STEALING CHICKENS AND EGGS. BUT EVEN THOUGH THAT IS A BAD THING FOR THE FARM, THEY ARE JUST TRYING TO SURVIVE AND FEED THEIR OWN CHILDREN! THEY USUALLY LIVE IN A FOXHOLE THAT HAS THREE ROOMS: THE ENTRANCE, WHERE THE MOTHER WILL SPEND HER TIME WATCHING OUTSIDE FOR PREY TO PASS NEARBY, A SECOND ROOM WHERE THEY STORE THEIR CAPTURED FOOD, AND A THIRD ROOM WHERE THE LITTLE ONES ARE BORN AND RAISED.

## COW

COWS ARE MEMBERS OF THE ANIMAL FAMILY CALLED **"RUMINANTS."** THIS FAMILY INCLUDES ANIMALS LIKE COWS, GOATS, SHEEP, DEER, AND CAMELS, WHO ALL HAVE FOUR STOMACHS! ACTUALLY, THEY ONLY HAVE ONE STOMACH, BUT THREE "PRE-STOMACHS" THAT PROCESS THE GRASS AND VEGETABLES BEFORE THEY EVEN REACH THE MAIN STOMACH. NORMALLY, AFTER A COW CHEWS AND SWALLOWS ITS FOOD, THE PRE-STOMACHS WILL BRING THE FOOD BACK UP INTO THE COW'S MOUTH TO CHEW AGAIN! EUGH, IT SOUNDS A LITTLE GROSS, BUT FOR MEMBERS OF THE COW FAMILY, THAT IS NORMAL! AND HERE'S AN INTERESTING FACT: A BULL FROM KANSAS HAS HORNS THAT ARE ALMOST 10 FEET LONG!

9.75 FEET! THAT'S HUGE!

THAT'S A WORLD RECORD!

SCRONTCH!
SCRONTCH!